DISCARD

Written by
KATSUHIRO OTOMO

Illustrated by
SHINJI KIMURA

translation by
KUMAR SIVASUBRAMANIAN

DH PRESS™

publisher
MIKE RICHARDSON

editor
CHRIS WARNER

original design
KATSUHIRO OTOMO

publication design
DEBRA BAILEY

art director
LIA RIBACCHI

published by
DH Press
A division of Dark Horse Comics, Inc.
10956 S.E. Main Street
Milwaukie OR 97222

dhpressbooks.com

First edition: August 2005
ISBN: 1-59582-002-7

10 9 8 7 6 5 4 3 2
Printed in U.S.A.

My name is Hipira.
The truth is, I'm a vampire!
Everybody had better be really afraid of me!

This is the town of Salta.
It's surrounded by a high, high wall,
and only vampires live here.
It's always nighttime here, and morning never comes,
so it's the kind of town kids dream about,
if they're the type who love to stay up late.

# The Tale of Soul

Right now in Salta,
there are lots of rumors going around
about the city's oldest "Town Elder"
and the mysteries of the castle he lives in.

There are always strange lights
beaming out from the castle's windows.

All right!
Time to explore!

Inside the castle,
there is a long, long set of stairs
that goes 'round and 'round
up the tower.

On the wall, portraits of the Town
Elder's father and grandfather...

...and their grandfathers
are all staring at me!
Yikes!

Now I'm right in front of the Elder's room.
Light is spilling out, and I can hear some
kind of magic spell being cast inside!
Let's take a peek and see...

I spent a hundred years collecting
the souls of humans, and now I'll
wring them out to make sprites.

If we drink the blood of
those sprites,
we vampires get
to go to hell.

'Cause when it comes to
vampires, hell is heaven!
Now watch, Hipira!

It looks like something's being created out of the tip of the vortex...

Heave-ho! Crank!
Quickly, Hipira!
Keep turning it!
AAH!

Come on... Just a little bit more, a little more...
All that's left is for it to sprout feet...
CRACK!!
We broke it...!

PLOP... The sprite tumbled to the
ground before it could grow legs!

Hi, my name's Soul.
Pleased to meet you!

But after that,
Hipira and Soul...

...became best friends.

# Cock-A-Doodle-Doo!

Hipira! Let's play!!

BWAH!

Scary, aren't I?

That's pretty funny, Hipira!

Cock-a-doodle-doo!

It's morning!!

AAH! It's Hipira!

Why, you--!

You stop that,
even in your dreams!

# The Frog Prince

This is the entrance to the forest at the back of the town of Salta. Hipira and Soul have come here to play.

Sniff sniff!
What's wrong?
Why are you crying?
I am
a briar pixie.
Sniff sniff.

The water of the river has stopped flowing,
so the oldest briar tree in the forest
is starting to wither up and die.

Hooray! Hooray!

It wasn't really the fault of some wizard at all. He just got big from drinking too much river water!

And he isn't a prince either!

He doesn't even look like a frog, does he?

# School Is Fun

Today Hipira is at
school studying.

Look! Even Hipira there is studying.

Oh! It's true! I can't believe it!

You see! Even Hipira does what he's supposed to, when he's been told!

THUMPTHUMPTHUMPTHUMP

# A New Friend

And so after that, sunglasses became all the rage in the town of Salta.

This is a major discovery. There's some kind of sprout coming out of that meteorite.

Look, Soul.

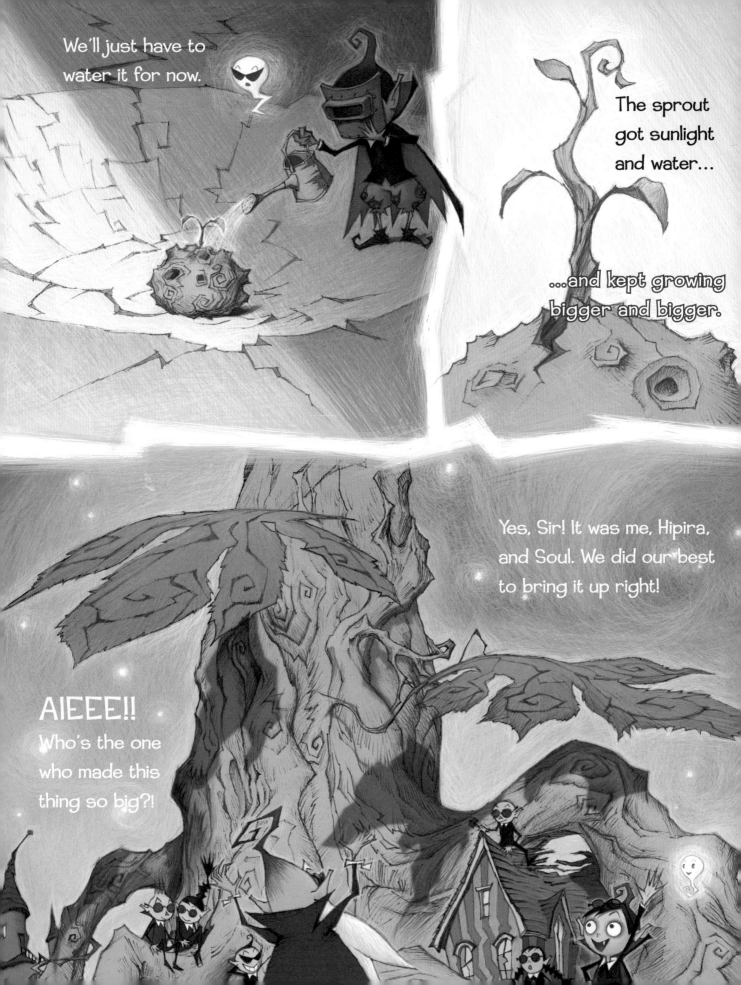

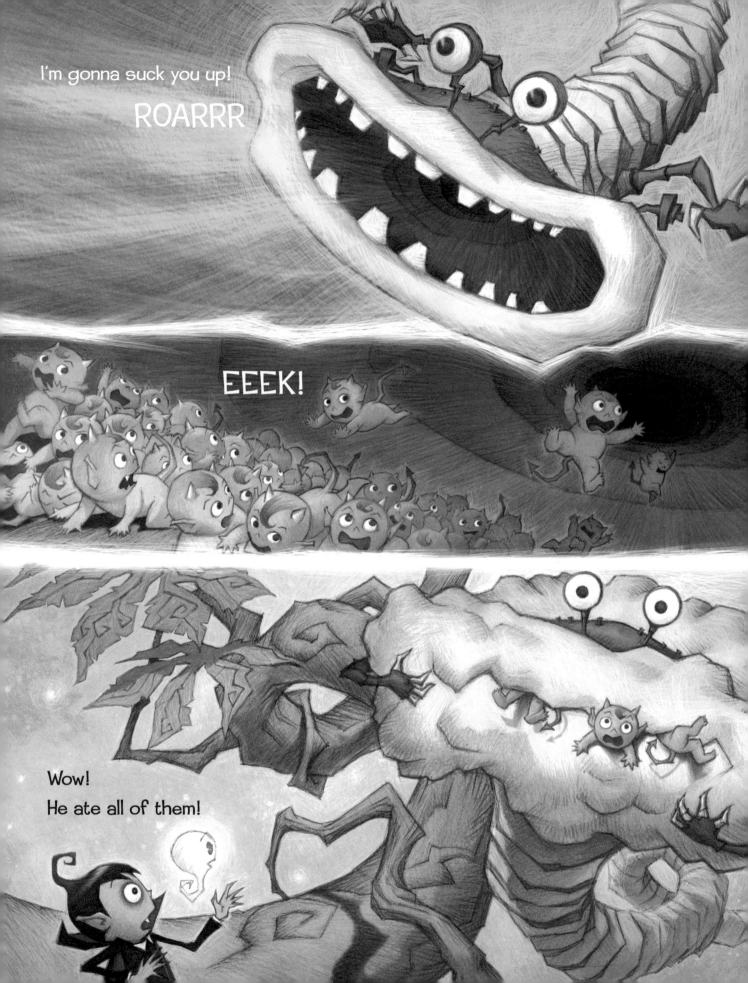

Well, we've got a new friend now,
don't we, Soul?

What should we name
him, Hipira...?

The End

**KATSUHIRO OTOMO** is known for his groundbreaking work as an artist, writer, and filmmaker. Otomo's graphic novel *Domu*, his major work, became a bestseller in Japan in 1983 and was the first manga to win the coveted Science Fiction Grand Prix Award, Japan's equivalent to America's Nebula Award. Upon completion of *Domu*, Otomo began work on *Akira*, an epic graphic novel that would be ten years in the making and would go on to win every possible award and become regarded as one of the crown jewels of graphic fiction. With the completion of *Akira*, Otomo began his odyssey as a filmmaker, directing the acclaimed animated *Akira* adaptation. Otomo has gone on to direct a number of films, both animated and live-action, and commercials. Otomo's latest film, *Steamboy*, is the most expensive film production in the history of Japanese animation. Otomo lives and works in Tokyo.

**SHINJI KIMURA** is one of Japan's most respected film production artists, creating dazzling background paintings and production designs for a number of popular animated films. Kimura began working at Kobayashi Productions and now works as a freelance artist/director. Some of his major credits in background art include *Urusei Yatsura 2: Beautiful Dreamer*, *Lupin the Third: The Plot of the Fuhma Clan*, and the beloved classic *My Neighbor Totoro*. Kimura met Katsuhiro Otomo as an art director on *Steamboy*, which led to their collaboration on *Hipira* . Kimura lives and works in Tokyo.